Maisy Goes to London

Lucy Cousins

WALKER BOOKS
AND SUBSIDIARIES

First stop, Piccadilly Circus.

Look at all the flashing lights!

Next they walk to Trafalgar Square
to see **Nelson's Column**. It's very tall!

"I love this big, friendly lion",
says Charley. **Maisy** snaps a photo.

click!

Then they go inside to look at all the paintings in the National Gallery.

There are so many amazing pictures.
Maisy likes the sunflowers best.

The palace guard is very serious.
He doesn't even smile.

Maisy takes another photo.

Next, they walk along the River Thames and see the Houses of Parliament.

Maisy and her friends
go on a river boat.

Look, the gates are opening
on Tower Bridge!

At the Tower of London,
Maisy takes some photos
of the ravens.

click!

Cyril and Charley love the Beefeater's colourful uniform.

Next,
they go
down, down, down
to the underground.

It's very crowded on the
tube train.
"Hold on tight!" says Maisy.

On the riverbank,
they buy some snacks. Yum!

Amazing! What a lot of fish!

"The shark's teeth look very sharp!" says Cyril.

Soon it's time to go,

but first they visit the **gift shop**.

Before they go home,
Maisy and her friends get one
last photo on the bridge.

click!

What a brilliant day!
"I LOVE London," says Maisy.

Piccadilly Circus

Nelson's Column

Tower Bridge

Hello, raven!